FIELD DAY FIASCO!

"Where's Mr. Jenkins?" Joe asked impatiently.

"Right there." Frank pointed to the gym teacher. He was jingling some keys and hurrying toward the shed door.

"Stand back, people," Mr. Jenkins called out cheerfully. "Let's do this in an organized fashion."

He stuck a key in the lock and swung open the shed door. But when he looked inside, he gasped.

"What's wrong?" a kid called out.

"This shed is a mess!" the teacher exclaimed. "It looks like someone tried to destroy the Field Day equipment!"

CATCH UP ON ALL THE HARDY BOYS® SECRET FILES

THE HARDY BOYS®

SECRET FILES #8

Sports Sabotage

BY FRANKLIN W. DIXON

ILLUSTRATED BY SCOTT BURROUGHS

ALADDIN • NEW YORK LONDON TORONTO SYDNEY NEW DELHI

ALADDIN

An imprint of Simon & Schuster Children's Publishing Division
1230 Avenue of the Americas, New York, NY 10020
First Aladdin paperback edition April 2012
Text copyright © 2012 by Simon & Schuster, Inc.
Illustrations copyright © 2012 by Scott Burroughs
All rights reserved, including the right of reproduction in whole or in part in any form.
ALADDIN is a trademark of Simon & Schuster, Inc., and related logo is a registered trademark of Simon & Schuster, Inc.
THE HARDY BOYS is a registered trademark of Simon & Schuster, Inc.
For information about special discounts for bulk purchases, please contact Simon & Schuster Special Sales at 1-866-506-1949 or business@simonandschuster.com.
The Simon & Schuster Speakers Bureau can bring authors to your live event. For more information or to book an event contact the Simon & Schuster Speakers Bureau at 1-866-248-3049 or visit our website at www.simonspeakers.com.
Designed by Lisa Vega
The text of this book was set in Garamond.
Manufactured in the United States of America 0115 OFF
10 9 8 7 6 5 4 3
Library of Congress Control Number 2011944990
ISBN 978-1-4424-2316-9
ISBN 978-1-4424-2317-6 (eBook)

CONTENTS

Sports Sabotage

1

An Exciting Event

Wait, Joe! Don't forget your carrot sticks," said the lunch lady.

Joe Hardy stopped. "Thanks," he said, grabbing the carrots and dropping them on his tray.

He rushed to catch up in the cafeteria line. He was in such a hurry that he accidentally bumped into the kid in front of him.

"Hey, watch it!" the kid said.

A teacher named Ms. Prentice was standing

nearby. She taught a different third-grade class from the one Joe was in.

"Is everything all right, boys?" she asked.

"Joe almost made me drop my tray." The other kid frowned at Joe.

"Sorry," Joe said. "I guess I wasn't paying attention."

"No harm done." Ms. Prentice smiled. "Just do your best not to destroy the cafeteria, all right, Joe?"

As soon as he was through the line, Joe hurried toward his usual table. His brother, Frank, was already there. So were their friends Phil, Iola, and Callie. They all had brown bag lunches in front of them.

Usually Joe brought lunch from home too. His aunt Gertrude, who lived with the Hardy family, made lunches for Joe and Frank every day. But today Joe had been so excited that he'd forgotten to grab his lunch on his way out of the house.

"The lunch line was superslow today," he said as he sat down. "What did I miss?"

Frank grinned. "Maybe we shouldn't tell you. That might teach you not to forget your lunch next time."

"Don't tease him, Frank," Iola said. "I don't blame Joe for being too excited to remember his lunch today. We're *all* excited that this Friday is Field Day!"

"I can't wait," Callie said. "We didn't have Field Day at my old school."

Callie had moved to Bayport recently. Even though she was new, she and Iola were already best friends.

"You'll love it," Iola told her.

Joe had just noticed that someone was missing. "Hey, where's Chet?" he asked. Chet Morton was Iola's brother and one of the Hardy brothers' best friends. He always sat with them at lunch.

"I'm not sure," Frank said. "He was in class this morning."

"He'd better get here soon or he'll miss lunch," Iola said, looking at Phil. "How long until we can go outside and practice?"

Phil checked his fancy digital watch. He always had all the latest high-tech gadgets.

"Twelve-and-a-half minutes until recess," he reported. "I think I'll practice for the sack race today." Each day that week at recess, students were allowed to practice for all the Field Day events.

"I'm going to work on the beanbag toss," Frank said.

"Don't bother. I'm going to win that one," Iola bragged. "And our class is going to beat yours for the class champion, too! Right, guys?"

"Yeah!" Joe cheered with a grin. He traded high fives with Iola and Callie. The three of them were all in the same class.

"No way," Frank said. "That grand prize is going to be ours!"

"Definitely," Phil agreed.

Joe noticed that Callie wasn't paying attention anymore. She was looking over at the next table.

"What are those guys doing?" she wondered.

Joe looked too. Three boys were sitting at the table. "Those are Adam's friends," Joe said. "So whatever they're doing, it's probably something obnoxious."

Adam Ackerman was the biggest bully at Bayport Elementary. He wasn't at the table right then. But his friends were bullies too. They were throwing popcorn at a boy standing nearby holding a lunch tray. One piece of popcorn went wide and landed in Joe's blond hair.

Joe brushed it away. "Looks like those jerks are harassing the new kid," he said. "Typical."

"Oh yeah, that guy just moved here," Iola said. "What's his name again? I think it's Tommy."

"No, it's Timmy." Callie stood up and waved. "Hey, Timmy! Come sit with us."

Timmy hurried over. He looked nervous but relieved. "Thanks," he said. "I wasn't sure where to sit."

Iola introduced Timmy to Frank and Phil. "They're fourth graders, but they're still pretty cool," she told him. "Even if we *are* going to crush them at Field Day."

"Dream on," Phil said with a laugh. "Us fourth graders are bigger, stronger, and faster than you third-grade twerps."

Timmy opened his milk carton. "I've been hearing about Field Day since I got here last week," he said. "I guess it's a pretty big deal, huh?"

Iola nodded. "It's superfun. Everyone can compete in as many games as they want. You get points for coming in first, second, or third. Whichever class has the most points at the end of the day wins a big party at Fun World!"

"What's Fun World?" Timmy asked.

"It's this cool place that has an arcade and batting cages and stuff," Frank explained.

"I heard Fun World is donating the grand prize too—two free passes to Fun World!" Phil looked at Timmy. "That's the prize for the person with the most points from the whole school."

"That'll be me," Iola bragged again. "I'm

planning to win everything I enter. Like the jump-roping contest, the beach ball keep-away, the water-balloon-and-spoon race, the relay race . . ."

"Don't forget the balloon stomp," Joe said. That was his favorite Field Day event. Each competitor got a balloon tied to his or her ankle. Then they all tried to break everyone else's balloons by stomping on them. "But you're not going to win that one—I am," Joe added. "The only one who beat me last year was Adam."

Phil nodded. "And that's only because he kept stomping on people's toes when the teachers weren't looking."

"Yeah," Joe said. "Anyway, I've been practicing all week. Watch my fancy footwork!"

As he jumped to his feet to demonstrate, his elbow hit his tray. It flew off the table and clattered to the floor with a loud *CRASH!*

"Nice technique, Joe," Iola said with a smirk.

Joe didn't answer. He'd just spotted Ms. Prentice rushing toward their table. She had an angry frown on her face.

"I think Ms. Prentice just saw you knock over your tray," Phil said to Joe.

"She saw me bump into someone earlier too," Joe remembered.

"She looks really mad," Callie whispered. "What if she gives you detention for the rest of the week? Then you won't be able to compete in Field Day!"

2

Recess Time

Frank held his breath as the teacher rushed over. If Joe couldn't take part in Field Day, it wouldn't be as much fun.

But Ms. Prentice strode right past without even looking at Joe. "Knock it off right this minute!" she scolded loudly, glaring at the next table. "I saw you boys throwing food just now."

Adam's friends scowled at her. "We weren't doing anything," one of them muttered.

"Whew!" Joe whispered. "I guess Ms. P. didn't see me drop my tray after all."

The teacher turned around. "Joe," she said, "I thought I asked you not to destroy the cafeteria. If you're this clumsy on Friday, you're going to have trouble winning anything at Field Day."

Frank and the others laughed. The teacher winked at Joe and walked away.

"Yikes!" Joe collapsed in his seat. "That was close."

Frank noticed someone hurrying through the cafeteria toward their table. "Here comes Chet," he said.

"It's about time." Iola waved at her older brother. "Hey, Chet! Hurry up or you won't have time to eat."

Phil checked his watch as Chet reached them. "Six-and-three-quarters minutes until recess," he reported.

Chet dropped his bag lunch on the table and collapsed into a chair. "I know!" he said breathlessly. "I lost track of the time."

"Where were you?" Frank asked.

"The science lab." Chet opened his lunch and pulled out a sandwich. "Mr. Sanchez said he'd show me how to take fingerprints with magnetic powder." He took a big bite of tuna salad, so his next words sounded muffled. "International spies do that kind of stuff all the time, you know."

Frank traded a look with his brother. Chet had been talking about spies nonstop for almost a week. It was his latest hobby. Chet had a *lot* of hobbies. But he usually only paid attention to each new hobby for a week or two before moving on to a different one.

"I'm going to try taking fingerprints at the park after school," Chet went on. "I want to see if the magnetic powder will work on different surfaces."

"That's nice." Iola turned toward Callie. "Who else should we ask to be on our team for the relay race?"

Chet frowned. "Are you guys still talking about Field Day?"

"Of course!" Joe grinned at him. "It's only two days away. Aren't you excited?"

"Not really." Chet rolled his eyes. "I'm not

exactly looking forward to getting my feet crushed again this year."

Frank remembered that Chet was one of the people whose feet Adam had stomped on last year. Besides that, Chet didn't like sports or running very much. It was no surprise he wasn't as excited about Field Day as the rest of them.

"Hey, Chet, maybe you should volunteer to help keep score this year," Phil suggested.

"That's a good idea," Callie agreed. "I heard Mr. Jenkins needs more volunteers. They won't be able to compete in any of the games, but they'll get some Fun World coupons as a reward for helping."

"Ugh." Joe made a face. "A few coupons sure wouldn't be enough to make *me* volunteer to miss all the fun!"

Chet nodded. "Yeah. I definitely don't want to do the balloon stomp this time. But I like doing the javelin throw with pool noodles. That's cool!"

They all talked about Field Day for the next few minutes. Finally the bell rang.

"Yay!" Joe cheered, pumping his fist. "Time for recess!"

He raced toward the exit. As he did he bumped into a girl with reddish-brown pigtails.

"Hey!" she complained.

But Joe was so eager to get outside that he didn't hear her. He didn't even notice he'd bumped into her.

Frank walked over to the girl. "Sorry about that, Rebecca," he said. "My brother's a little excited about practicing for Field Day."

Rebecca rolled her eyes. "I wish everyone would stop talking about stupid Field Day all the time."

Callie and Iola had caught up with Frank by then. "Stupid?!" Iola said in surprise. "Why do you think Field Day is stupid?"

Rebecca shrugged and didn't answer. Frank

spotted Phil and Chet disappearing through the door after Joe.

"Anyway, sorry again about my brother," he told Rebecca. Then he, Iola, and Callie headed outside.

"What's with her?" Iola wondered aloud, glancing back at Rebecca.

"She seems pretty quiet and shy," Callie said. "And she's always trying to get out of doing stuff in gym class."

"That's true," Iola said. "She hates sports. I guess it's no wonder she's not excited about Field Day."

Frank laughed. "Compared to Rebecca, I guess Chet looks like the world's biggest Field Day fan!"

They caught up with Joe, Chet, and Phil halfway to the equipment shed by the playing fields. That was where the Field Day equipment was stored. A bunch of other kids were milling around there too.

"Where's Mr. Jenkins?" Joe asked impatiently.

"Right there." Frank pointed to the gym

teacher. He was jingling some keys and hurrying toward the shed door.

"Stand back, people," Mr. Jenkins called out cheerfully. "Let's do this in an organized fashion."

But when he got to the shed door, he gasped. The front window was smashed!

"What's wrong?" a kid called out.

"Someone broke into the shed!" the teacher exclaimed. "And it looks like someone tried to destroy the Field Day equipment!"

3

What a Mess!

Joe shoved his way to the front of the crowd around the shed. "What do you mean? What's wrong with the Field Day stuff?" he exclaimed.

He stepped carefully around the broken glass and looked into the shed. Mr. Jenkins was right— the inside was a mess! Yesterday the Field Day equipment had been stacked neatly on shelves. Now it was thrown all over the place!

But Joe only got a quick look before the gym

teacher closed the door. "Back off, everyone," Mr. Jenkins ordered as he locked the door. "I'd better go tell Principal Butler what happened."

He hurried toward the school building, frowning.

"Wow," Joe said as he rejoined Frank and the others. "This is crazy. Who would mess up the equipment like that?"

"I don't know," Frank said. "Let's look for clues."

"That's a great idea," Iola said. "You guys have solved lots of other mysteries. You can solve this one, too!"

Phil and Callie nodded. The Hardy brothers were becoming well-known around Bayport as amateur detectives. They'd learned all about solving mysteries from their father, a private investigator.

Only Chet looked dubious. "Do you really

think there's a mystery here?" he said. "I bet it was raccoons."

"What do you mean?" Callie asked.

"Everyone knows that the school has had problems with raccoons getting into the trash and making a big mess," Chet said.

"Yeah, but the trash bins are outside," Phil pointed out. "How would raccoons get into a locked shed?"

"Easy," Chet said. "I'm saving up my money to buy this cool spy stuff I saw in a magazine. If I were a spy trying to break in here, I'd use this high-tech tool to break the glass in the windows." He shrugged. "But a raccoon could probably get in if it hit it enough with its claws."

Joe rolled his eyes. Sometimes Chet got so caught up in his hobbies that he forgot about everything else. "Well, I got a pretty good look at the damaged equipment," Joe said. "It didn't look like something an animal would do."

"We should investigate just in case," Frank agreed. "But Chet might be right about the raccoons. I mean, what person would want to ruin the equipment?"

"Yeah," Iola said, "the whole school is excited about Field Day!"

Frank looked thoughtful. "Well, not the *whole* school," he said. "What about Rebecca?"

"That weird, quiet girl?" Joe asked. "What about her?"

"You almost knocked her over when you were rushing out here," Iola informed him. "Frank had to stop and apologize for you."

Frank nodded. "When we mentioned Field Day, she said it was stupid." He pointed to Chet. "And we know Chet isn't that excited about it either. There are probably other people like that. Maybe even some who are willing to ruin things for everyone."

That made Joe think of someone. "I bet it was Adam Ackerman. He's mean enough to do something like this."

"Adam?" Frank looked doubtful. "Why would he want to ruin Field Day? He always wins a ton of events."

"Everyone thinks he's probably going to win the grand prize this year," Phil said.

"No way," Iola put in. "I'm going to win!"

"Nope, it's going to be me," Joe argued.

Just then Mr. Jenkins came hurrying back. The school principal, Ms. Butler, was right behind him. Both of them looked very serious.

"Listen up, people," Principal Butler said to all the kids. "Please clear this area while Mr. Jenkins and I have a look around. You may continue recess over on the playground."

"But what about practicing for Field Day?" a kid complained.

The principal traded a look with the gym teacher. "We'll let you know what's happening in a few minutes," Principal Butler said.

Joe wandered toward the playground with everyone else. "What do you think they're going to do?" he asked.

"I don't know," Phil said. "I guess we'll have to wait and find out."

Joe sighed. He hated waiting.

"Even if I can't use any of the Field Day stuff, at least I can still practice for the chin-up competition," he declared. Racing over to the monkey bars, he grabbed the highest bar he could reach. Then he swung himself even higher until he was hanging off the top rails.

Phil and Chet went past the monkey bars to the seesaws, while the two girls walked toward the swings. But Frank followed his brother, climbing up until he was hanging right beside him.

"I wish we could get a better look inside that shed," Frank said.

"I know what you mean." Joe did a few chin-ups, then stopped to rest. "We might be able to find some clues."

"Right. And then we could start figuring out the *W*s," Frank said.

"Who, What, When, Where, Why, and How," Joe recited, doing a chin-up for each word. Their father had taught them that those were the questions they should try to figure out for each case they wanted to solve.

Frank hooked his knees over the bar so he was hanging upside down. "We already know the answer to one of them: Where," he said.

"Yeah, that part's obvious," Joe replied. "We also know What—that someone messed up the Field Day equipment."

"We kind of know When," Frank went on. "At least, we know the stuff was fine at recess yesterday."

"So now we need to figure out Who, Why, and How," Joe said.

They were still talking about the case a few minutes later when Principal Butler came to the playground and called for attention. Joe stopped doing chin-ups and jumped to the ground. Everyone else stopped what they were doing and turned to listen too.

"Mr. Jenkins and I are convinced that someone vandalized the equipment shed on purpose," the principal announced with a frown. "Please come to my office right away if you want to confess, or if you have any idea who might have done it. If nobody comes forward before the end of the day tomorrow, Field Day will be canceled!"

4

Clues in the Shed

Frank checked the clock on the classroom wall. The school day would be over in five minutes, and the mystery of the messed-up shed was still unsolved. That left only twenty-four hours to figure out who'd done it, or Field Day would be canceled.

After her announcement, Principal Butler had ordered everyone to stay away from the equipment shed. That meant Frank and Joe hadn't been able to look for any clues. How were they supposed to solve the mystery if they couldn't check out the scene of the crime?

Frank had been thinking about that question all afternoon. Now he thought he'd come up with an answer.

Finally the bell rang. Frank grabbed his backpack and rushed for the door.

"Hey, wait up!" Chet said, jogging after him. "Why are you in such a hurry?"

Frank paused to let him catch up. "I have an idea about how Joe and I can get into that shed."

"Me too," Chet said. "Except I don't have enough money to get that spy watch yet."

"We don't need a spy watch," Frank said. "I have a plan."

"Really? What is it?"

"I don't have time to explain." Frank hurried into the hall. "I need to get Joe."

"Can I come too?" Chet asked. "I might be

useful. I know a lot about solving crimes now that I'm studying international espionage."

"Sure, you can come. But hurry!"

Joe was stepping out of his classroom when Frank and Chet arrived. Frank grabbed his brother's arm.

"Where are we going?" Joe asked as Frank dragged him down the hall.

"The gym," Frank said. "You'll see why in a second."

They reached the gym just as Mr. Jenkins was heading for the door. "Hello, boys," the gym teacher said when he saw them. "Can I help you?"

"No sir," Frank said. "But we'd like to help *you*. That equipment shed looked like a real mess. Do you need help cleaning it up?"

Mr. Jenkins smiled. "Thank you, Frank," he said. "As a matter of fact, I was just heading out there to start straightening up. I could use some help if you boys are willing. I'm hoping whoever sabotaged the shed will confess in time to save Field Day."

"Does that mean nobody has confessed yet?" Joe asked.

"Not yet," the gym teacher said with a sigh.

"But I'd like to have the equipment ready to go, just in case."

The three boys watched Mr. Jenkins open the shed. Frank stepped forward as soon as the door swung open. He wanted to get a good look inside before anyone touched anything.

It was even messier than Frank had realized. Tangled jump ropes and deflated beach balls were in a messy pile on the floor. Several pool noodles had been ripped up and flung around. Marbles were scattered everywhere, and uninflated balloons were stomped into the shed's floor.

"Wow," Chet said. "Those raccoons must've been really mad!"

"Raccoons?" Mr. Jenkins echoed. "Sorry, Chet. I don't think raccoons could do this much damage in such a short period of time."

"What do you mean?" Frank asked. "Do you know when it happened?"

"Yes—during lunch period," Mr. Jenkins replied. "I was out here just before that, and everything was fine."

Frank traded a look with his brother. This was an important clue!

"They got in through the smashed window," Frank said.

"And no one was around to notice," Joe added.

Mr. Jenkins nodded. "Anyone could have climbed into the shed that way," he agreed. "Now, shall we get started, boys?"

Soon Frank, Joe, and Chet were hard at work cleaning up the shed. While he picked up marbles and the pieces of ripped-up pool noodles, Frank kept his eyes open for clues.

After a few minutes Mr. Jenkins left to get more trash bags. Joe was looking outside the shed for more clues. Chet was putting beanbags into a box near where Frank was working.

"Have you found any clues yet?" Chet asked Frank.

"No. But at least now we have a better answer to one of our *W*s: When."

"You mean because of what Mr. Jenkins said?" Chet's box of beanbags was full. He picked it up and looked around for a clear shelf to set it on. "It might be useful to feed that information into some spy software." He shrugged. "You know—if we had any."

Frank hardly heard him. "The crime definitely happened during lunch period," he said thoughtfully. "That means anyone who was in the cafeteria all during lunch couldn't have done it."

Just then Joe let out a shout. "Get out here!" he called. "There's a footprint outside the shed."

Frank felt his heart jump. This could be another important clue! "Coming!" he said, dropping

the ripped balloons he was holding and rushing
toward his brother.

"Do you think it belongs to the bad guy?"
Chet exclaimed. "Too bad I don't have my spy
watch yet. It includes a special spy-quality hidden
cam—oof!"

Chet had just stepped on a batch of marbles

still lying on the floor. He lost his balance and went flying. The box of beanbags flew out of his hands—straight toward Joe.

"Hey!" Joe stumbled back just in time to keep from getting creamed by the beanbags.

Instead, they fell outside the shed—right over the footprint!

5

The Eavesdropper

I still can't believe I wrecked that footprint." Chet sighed loudly, kicking at a stone on the sidewalk. "It was our only clue!"

"Forget about it," Joe told him. He'd been mad at first when Chet's clumsiness had ruined the footprint. Once the boys had cleared away the beanbags, they couldn't see any sign of the print anymore.

But Chet couldn't help being clumsy. There was

no point staying mad at him. Now Joe, Chet, and Frank were discussing the mystery as they walked toward the park.

"Are you sure you didn't see anything unusual about the footprint?" Frank asked.

Joe shook his head. "I already told you—it looked like it was left by a kid-size sneaker. That's all I noticed before I called you guys over."

"That doesn't narrow things down much." Frank glanced at the others' feet as they walked. "Most of the kids in school wear sneakers. Including all three of us."

"Too bad we don't have infrared heat-sensing equipment or something," Chet said. "If we did, we could use it to track whoever left that footprint, and . . ."

Joe didn't pay much attention as Chet rambled on and on about spy stuff. What was the point of talking about what an international superspy would do? Spies had all kinds of crazy equipment that normal people didn't.

When they reached the park, Phil, Iola, and Callie were already there. So was Timmy. He and Phil were watching the two girls practice for the three-legged race.

"Hi," Iola said when the Hardys and Chet walked over. "Did you guys solve the case?"

"Not yet," Frank said.

"We're working on it, though," Chet said.

"I thought you decided raccoons did it," Phil said to him.

Chet shrugged. "That's one of my theories. But a good spy never rules anything out."

"What are you talking about?" Timmy sounded confused. "Are you really a spy?"

"Chet's not a spy except in his own mind." Iola rolled her eyes. "But Frank and Joe are detectives for real."

"Detectives?" Timmy glanced at the brothers, looking unsure. "Really?"

"Yeah," Phil said. "They've solved tons of cases. Like when this kid's baseball mitt went missing, or the time Adam Ackerman stole some money at Fun World, or—"

"That reminds me," Joe interrupted. "I think Adam should be number one on our suspect list. Even though he loves Field Day, he's the only person who's rotten enough to want to ruin it for everyone else."

Joe expected Frank to argue. He usually did when Joe wanted to put Adam on one of their suspect lists—mostly because Joe *always* wanted to put Adam on their suspect lists. But this time Frank looked thoughtful.

"Did anyone notice whether Adam was at lunch today?" he asked.

Iola made a face. "I try not to notice Adam anytime."

"No, I'm serious," Frank said. "We found out that whoever messed up the shed did it during lunch. Mr. Jenkins said the shed was fine right before that."

Phil's eyes widened. "Adam wasn't at lunch today. I noticed it because his stupid friends were acting even stupider than usual."

"You're right," Iola agreed.

"That proves it!" Joe exclaimed. "Adam wasn't in the cafeteria because he was outside messing up the shed!"

"Wait," Callie said. "I just remembered something. Adam has detention all week. I saw him in the office when my mom came to pick me up for a dentist appointment yesterday right after school."

"Really? What'd he do this time?" Joe asked.

"I don't know—he wouldn't say," Callie said.

Iola rolled her eyes. "He probably called one of the teachers a dummy again."

"He wouldn't get a whole week for that," Phil pointed out. "It had to be something worse."

Joe noticed that Timmy was listening but not saying anything. "Adam Ackerman is that kid in our class who's always getting in trouble," Joe told the new kid. "He gets detention a lot."

"Yeah," Chet said. "That means he has to sit in the principal's office during lunch, recess, and after school."

"So I guess that means he's got an alibi for this crime," Frank said.

"Huh?" Joe said. Then he thought about it. "Oh yeah," he added. "Ms. Chou never takes her eyes off the kids in detention."

"Who's Ms. Chou?" Timmy asked. "I thought the principal was Ms. Butler."

"Ms. Chou is the school secretary," Iola explained. "She's in charge of detention, and she's nice but tough. Nobody messes with her—not even Adam."

"Oh well," Joe said. "Guess we'll have to come up with some different suspects."

They kept talking about the case and practicing for Field Day until it was time to head home for dinner. "See you guys tomorrow," Phil said. "I hope you solve the mystery by then."

"Yeah," Iola agreed. "It would stink if Field Day got canceled."

Joe waved to his friends, then followed his brother toward the path through the woods that led to their neighborhood.

"We really need some new suspects," Frank said as they walked down the winding, shady trail. "Can you think of any?"

Joe shrugged. "Just those raccoons Chet keeps

talking about. But I still don't think animals did all that stuff."

"Me neither. Especially since you found that *human* footprint by the window." Frank thought for a second. "We need to figure out why someone would do something like this. What's the motive?"

"Trying to get Field Day canceled, I guess," Joe said. "Except I can't imagine anyone wanting to do that."

"Not everybody loves Field Day," Frank reminded him. "That girl Rebecca, for instance. Maybe she should be on our list."

"Maybe. It's hard to imagine her ripping up pool noodles and throwing stuff around." Joe made a face. Rebecca was the type of girl who never wanted to get her hands dirty or do anything fun. "Hey! If we're putting Rebecca on the list, how about Chet?" he joked. "He's not crazy about Field Day either."

"Chet? Yeah, right," Frank said with a laugh.

Joe knew Chet would never, ever do something so rotten. But it was funny to think about. After all, he'd make a pretty good suspect if they didn't know better.

"It all makes perfect sense," he said in a loud, dramatic voice. "Chet *must* have done it! He doesn't like Field Day—he said so at lunch today, remember?"

Frank grinned, playing along. "And he *did* miss more than half of today's lunch period," he said. "Maybe he was out using his superspy skills to break into the equipment shed."

"Right," Joe said. "And he ruined our only clue just now. He *claimed* it was an accident, but who knows?"

"Plus, he keeps trying to convince everyone that raccoons did it," Frank said. "He's framing those poor, innocent raccoons!"

Both brothers were cracking up by now. But

Joe stopped laughing when he heard rustling in the woods nearby.

"Did you hear that?" He saw someone dart behind a tree. "Hey! Who's there?"

A figure stepped into view. Adam Ackerman!

"Hi, nerds," Adam said.

"Aren't you supposed to be in detention?" Frank asked.

Adam rolled his eyes. "Can't you tell time? Detention's only for an hour after school."

"What are you doing sneaking around out here?" Joe demanded.

"None of your beeswax." Adam sneered. "It's a free country—I can walk wherever I want."

"Yeah, so can we," Frank said. "And we're walking away from you."

Frank hurried down the trail with Joe right behind him. Joe looked back a couple of times, but Adam didn't try to follow them.

"Do you think he was spying on us?" Joe asked.

Frank smiled. "Now you sound like Chet. Anyway, it doesn't matter if Adam heard us talking. He can't be the bad guy this time, remember? He has an airtight alibi."

"I wish we had some good suspects," Joe said as he and Frank climbed off the bus the next morning. "We only have until the end of today to solve the case."

They went into the school building. A bunch of kids nearby were laughing and high-fiving.

"What's going on?" Joe asked them.

"Field Day's back on!" one of the kids exclaimed.

Just then Phil came rushing toward them. He didn't look as happy as the others. In fact, he was frowning.

"What's wrong?" Joe asked. "Didn't you hear the good news? Field Day's back on!"

"Yeah," Frank said. "I guess someone confessed."

"Not exactly," Phil said grimly. "But Ms. Butler thinks she knows who did it. "

"Really? Who?" Joe asked.

"Chet."

6

Alibis and Excuses

Frank could hardly believe his ears. "Chet?!" he exclaimed. "No way!"

"Someone accused him," Phil said. "Ms. Butler didn't believe it at first. But she made Chet open his locker, and there were a bunch of Field Day balloons in there."

"What?" Joe shook his head. "This doesn't make sense!"

"You're right." Frank's logical mind was already working on the problem. "Chet has an alibi, remember? He was with Mr. Sanchez during most of lunch, then with us for the rest."

"You're right!" Joe cried. "Chet definitely couldn't have done it. Didn't he tell Ms. Butler that? Let's go find him!"

They all rushed to Chet's classroom. Most kids were still out on the playground or in the halls. But Chet was sitting at his desk looking miserable.

"We heard what happened," Frank said. "Don't worry, we know you're innocent."

"And so does Mr. Sanchez," Joe put in. "You need to go talk to him. He can tell Ms. Butler that

you were with him while the shed was getting messed up."

Chet bit his lip. "That's the problem," he said softly. "I wasn't."

"Huh?" Joe blinked. "What do you mean? You told us—"

"I know," Chet said. "And I really did go see Mr. Sanchez and get that fingerprint powder. But then he had to leave to do something else, and I spent a while in the lab by myself messing around with the powder." He shrugged. "I stayed there until my stomach started growling and I realized lunch was more than half over."

Frank felt his heart sink. "So nobody else saw you in the science lab after Mr. Sanchez left?"

Chet shook his head. "But I *was* there—I swear!"

"We believe you," Joe said, while Frank and Phil nodded.

"The trouble is, there's no way to prove it,"

Frank said. "You don't have an alibi. And since Principal Butler found those balloons in your locker . . ."

"Yeah, where'd those balloons come from?" Joe asked.

"I don't know." Chet sounded more miserable than ever. He sniffled. "I'm glad you guys believe I'm innocent. I just hope my parents believe it too. Ms. Butler said she's going to call them at the end of the day if I haven't confessed by then."

"That doesn't give us much time." Frank glanced at his brother. "Let's go start investigating."

Phil stayed behind with Chet while Frank and Joe hurried out into the hallway. "Now I *really* wish we had more suspects," Joe said.

"Me too," Frank said. "But I guess we'd better start with the only one on the list."

"Who? You mean Rebecca? She's not much of a suspect."

"I know. But you know what Dad says—it's important to follow up on every lead, clue, or hunch." Frank headed down the hall. "Let's go question her."

They found Rebecca at her locker. She was humming a cheerful tune as she grabbed a snack that was inside.

"Hi," Frank greeted her. "Can we talk to you for a second?"

She turned around. "Sure, it's a free country."

Frank noticed that she didn't sound grumpy, like she had yesterday. Today she seemed to be in a much better mood. Could that be because she was relieved that Chet had been accused of her crime?

"Why do you hate Field Day so much?" Joe demanded.

Rebecca looked surprised. "I don't hate it *that* much," she said. "At least, not anymore."

"What do you mean?" Frank asked. "Yesterday you wanted everyone to stop talking about it."

"I did?" She shrugged. "I guess that was before Mr. Jenkins said I could be a scorekeeper."

"Huh?" Joe said. "Wait, you mean you actually volunteered to keep track of the scores and stuff instead of competing?"

"That's right," Rebecca said with a smile. "It's going to be cool! We all get coupons to Fun World, plus Mr. Jenkins is taking us out for pizza afterward. Now I'm actually looking forward to Field Day!"

Joe still looked doubtful.

But Frank remembered that Rebecca didn't like gym class or sports. She probably really thought that being a scorekeeper at Field Day was better than competing in the games, even if Frank, Joe, and practically everyone else in school disagreed.

"That's cool," he said. "Um, we have to go now. Come on, Joe."

He dragged his brother off and explained what he was thinking as they walked down the hall. It was almost time for class to start by then, so only a few kids were still wandering around or grabbing stuff out of their lockers.

"How do you know she's telling the truth?" Joe said. "Maybe she's just faking being excited about Field Day so we won't suspect her. She could've stuck those balloons into Chet's locker through the vents to frame him."

"But why Chet? He's never done anything to her. They barely even know each other." Frank shook his head, feeling frustrated. "It doesn't make sense. I feel like we're missing something, like an important clue or fact or—"

"Look!" Joe grabbed his arm as they rounded a corner. "There—at Chet's locker!"

Frank looked where his brother was pointing. Someone was standing in front of Chet's locker. But it wasn't Chet. It was the new kid, Timmy.

"Hey!" Joe blurted out. "What are you doing?"

Timmy jerked back and spun around, his eyes wide and startled. Then he turned and dashed away in the opposite direction!

7

A New Suspect?

Stop!" Joe shouted, racing after Timmy. "Timmy, we saw you!"

After a few steps Timmy stopped. "Oh!" he said, turning around with a sheepish smile. "Hi, Joe. Hi, Frank. You guys scared me. I thought you were a teacher yelling at me 'cause I was late for class!"

Frank skidded to a stop behind Joe. "You *are* almost late," he told Timmy. "What were you doing at Chet's locker?"

"Was that Chet's locker?" Timmy laughed. "Sorry, I thought it was mine. This school is a lot different from my old one."

Just then a teacher stuck her head out into the hallway. "Hurry along, boys," she said sternly. "The late bell is about to ring."

"Oops, she's right. See you guys later!" Timmy waved and took off toward his class.

Frank and Joe walked after him more slowly. "Do you think he was telling the truth?" Joe asked.

"Maybe," Frank said. "After all, he *is* new— it makes sense that he'd still be finding his way around. But it's kind of suspicious."

"Yeah," Joe agreed. "Especially since he was late to lunch yesterday. Remember?"

Frank nodded. "What if he was the one who put those balloons in Chet's locker before?" he said. "I guess we'd better add him to our suspect list."

Joe agreed, feeling troubled. He'd been hoping

they might figure out a new suspect for the case. But he hadn't expected it to be someone who seemed as nice as Timmy. "I guess you're right," he said as they reached the door to his class. "See you at lunch. Maybe we can question him more then."

"Hey, Timmy," Joe said casually as he unwrapped his sandwich. "Why were you so late to lunch yesterday?"

Timmy glanced up from his food. He'd brought a brown bag lunch today, just like the others.

"I was talking to Ms. Walsh," he said. "I stayed

behind to ask her about fractions. You guys are ahead of where we were at my old school."

"No wonder you were late," Iola said with a laugh. "Ms. Walsh *loves* talking about fractions!"

"Yeah," Chet agreed. "She'd talk about them all day if she could."

"She does," Phil pointed out. "She *teaches* them all day, remember?"

Joe wasn't sure whether to feel relieved or disappointed. He was glad that Timmy had an alibi. But this meant they were all out of suspects again.

"I think I'll go buy some juice," Frank announced. "Want to come, Joe?"

"No thanks, I'm not thirsty." Joe couldn't believe his brother was thinking about juice at a time like this.

"Are you sure?" Frank glared at him.

Finally Joe caught on. His brother wanted to talk in private about what Timmy had just told them.

"Oh!" He hopped to his feet. "Come to think of it, I need, uh, some napkins."

Their friends didn't pay any attention as the brothers hurried away. Frank led the way to a private spot near the recycling bins.

"So that's one more person with an alibi," Frank said.

"Yeah." Joe sighed. "Too bad Chet doesn't have one."

"I know. That means the only way to clear his name is to figure out who *really* did it," Frank said. "Let's think about our *W*s. We already know *when* the crime happened, right? We just need to figure out *who* could have done it during that time."

Joe nodded. "Most people have an easy alibi for the time it happened—they were in the cafeteria where everyone could see them."

"Plus there are a few others, like Adam and Timmy, who have other alibis," Frank added. "We need to ask around and find out who doesn't have an alibi at all."

"Right." Joe felt better just having a plan. "Then what are we waiting for? Let's go!"

"Are you *sure* you were *all* here the whole time yesterday?" Joe asked.

The table full of girls stared at him. "Duh," one girl said. "Didn't we just say that?"

"Even Rebecca?" Joe added, glancing at the girl with the reddish-brown braids. "She was here all through lunch?"

One of the other girls giggled. "Why, do you want to ask her out or something?" she teased.

"Shut up," Rebecca said, her cheeks going pink.

"Whatever," Joe muttered.

He hurried away from the girls' table. So far he hadn't found out anything interesting. He looked around, trying to decide where to go next.

He was near the table where Adam's three friends were sitting. Their names were Jeffrey, Joe, and Ian. For a second, Joe thought about skipping that table. Those guys were just as likely to dump their food on his head as they were to answer his questions.

But he knew what Frank would say. They had to talk to everyone if they wanted to clear Chet's name *and* save Field Day.

Doing his best to look confident, he walked over. "Hi," he said.

"What do you want?" Ian demanded.

He sounded kind of crabby. The other two looked unhappy too.

"What's wrong with you guys?" Joe asked. "Aren't you excited that it's almost Field Day?"

"Why should we be excited?" Joe said with a scowl. "Our class is going to lose this year."

"Yeah," Jeffrey added. "And it's all you-know-who's fault!"

All three of them turned and glared at someone across the cafeteria. Joe tried to follow their gazes, but he couldn't tell who they were looking at.

"What are you talking about?" he asked. "Whose fault?"

"None of your beeswax," Ian growled. "Now scram, nerd!"

Then Joe thought of a better question. "Anyway, how is someone going to make your class lose?"

"Duh!" Jeffrey said angrily. "By getting Adam banned from Field Day!"

8

More Alibis

Frank was standing near the cafeteria exit, thinking hard, when Joe rushed over.

"Guess what I just found out?" Joe exclaimed breathlessly.

"Did someone confess?" Frank asked hopefully.

"No—it's about Adam." Joe looked around to make sure nobody was close enough to hear him. "He's banned from Field Day this year!"

"He is? Oh, right—he has detention all week.

That means he can't do Field Day." Frank shrugged. "So what?"

"So his friends are really mad at someone—I guess whoever got him in trouble. They wouldn't tell me who, though."

"It doesn't matter," Frank reminded him. "Adam couldn't have messed up the shed—he was in detention when it happened."

"Yeah, I know," Joe said. "I just thought it was interesting. Did you find anybody without an alibi yet?"

"Not really," Frank said. "I found one person who missed lunch yesterday for a doctor's appointment. Another kid was late because she had to go to the nurse's office to take her allergy medicine."

"So they have alibis, just like everyone else." Joe sighed. "Except Chet."

"That's what I've been thinking about." Frank stuck his hands in his pockets. "Why Chet?"

"Why doesn't he have an alibi?" Joe rolled his eyes. "Because he's Chet. He's always getting caught up in his hobbies and forgetting about everything else."

"That's not what I mean," Frank said. "I mean, why would someone decide to frame *Chet* for the crime? Wouldn't it make more sense to pick someone who was a troublemaker to begin with—like Adam?"

"Sure," Joe said. "But he has an alibi. You just said so."

"That's what's bugging me. We've been investigating for two days and we still don't know exactly who has an alibi and who doesn't. But somehow, someone figured out that Chet doesn't have one."

Joe gasped. "Adam!" he exclaimed.

Frank sighed. Joe really had a one-track mind sometimes. "We already know Adam couldn't have—"

"No, wait!" Joe sounded excited now. "I just remembered something. Adam was skulking around in the woods when we were walking home yesterday, remember?"

"Yeah. So?"

"So what if he heard us joking around about how Chet would make such a great suspect, including the part about how he was late to lunch?" Joe said. "He could've told his rotten friends about it. Maybe they're the ones who wrecked the shed because they were mad about Adam getting banned from Field Day!"

For a second Frank was excited too. Had Joe just solved the mystery?

Then he remembered something. "Adam's friends couldn't have done it," he reminded Joe. "They were definitely at lunch yesterday—we saw them ourselves, remember? They were throwing stuff at Timmy and then Ms. Prentice yelled at them."

"Are you sure they were there the whole time?" Joe asked. "Even before I got there?"

Frank nodded. "I'm

sure. We could hear them being obnoxious from the second we all sat down. There's no way any of them sneaked out long enough to wreck the shed."

Joe's shoulders slumped. "Oh well," he said, kicking at a crumpled napkin on the floor. "I guess we still don't have any clues or suspects."

But Frank was thinking again. "I'm not so sure about that," he said. "Like I said before, Dad always tells us to follow up on every lead, clue, or hunch."

"Isn't that what we've been doing?" Joe asked.

"Not quite," Frank said. "We never double-checked to make sure Adam really has detention."

"But Callie said . . . ," Joe began.

"I know. And I'm definitely not saying she's lying." Frank shrugged. "But what if Adam got out early for some reason yesterday? We should check with Ms. Chou just in case. We can go talk to her during recess."

"Okay, I guess." Joe didn't look very happy

about missing part of recess. "Come on, we'd better get back to our food."

Back at their table, everyone looked upset. "What's going on?" Frank asked.

Iola shot a dirty look at the table where Adam's friends were sitting. "Those idiots are throwing peas at us," she complained.

"Incoming!" Ian shouted. A second later a pea splatted against Timmy's forehead.

"Stop that!" Iola hollered.

She had a pretty loud voice. Ms. Prentice looked over from her spot near the cafeteria line just as Joe tossed another handful of peas. The teacher frowned and stormed over.

"Good!" Phil said as the teacher yelled at the other boys. "Maybe now they'll leave us alone for a while."

"Are you okay?" Callie asked Timmy. "It looks like most of the peas hit you."

"I'm fine." Timmy brushed a pea off his lap. "It's no big deal."

Chet wasn't paying much attention to the others. "Did you solve the mystery yet?" he asked Frank and Joe hopefully.

"Not yet," Frank replied. "But we're working on it."

Chet's face crumpled. "This is terrible!" he exclaimed. "If you don't figure it out by the end of today, Principal Butler will call my parents!"

"Mom and Dad will believe your side of the story," Iola said.

"What if they don't?" Chet sounded more upset with every word. "What if they think I did it? They might not let me order that spy watch!"

"Don't worry, Chet," Joe said. "We'll figure out who framed you. We promise!"

"Really?" Chet sounded a tiny bit less upset.

"Sure," Frank said. But secretly, he hoped he and Joe would be able to keep that promise. With no clues and no suspects, it wasn't going to be easy.

9

Double-Checking

Let's hurry, okay?" Joe glanced over his shoulder at his friends, who were heading outside for recess. "I want to practice the beanbag toss so I can beat Iola tomorrow."

"Just come on." Frank headed in the opposite direction. "We need to figure out this mystery. If we don't prove Chet didn't do it, none of us will have any fun at Field Day."

Joe realized his brother was right. They couldn't let Chet take the blame. Besides, if there was even a slight chance that Adam was behind the trouble, Joe definitely wanted to prove it.

The office was right down the hall from the cafeteria. It had big glass windows and glass doors. Inside, Joe could see Ms. Chou sitting behind a long countertop. Behind her was the door leading into Principal Butler's office. At the far end of the room was the space where kids sat for detention. There were several tables and chairs over there, but only one was occupied. Adam was slouched there picking at his fingernails, looking sullen and bored.

Ms. Chou looked up when Frank and Joe entered. "Well, well!" she said cheerfully. "It's my favorite brothers."

Joe smiled. Ms. Chou called everyone her "favorite." "Hi, Ms. Chou," he said. "We have a question for you." He glanced toward Adam, who had looked up by then and was staring at them. "It's kind of private," Joe added.

Ms. Chou raised one eyebrow. "Oh, I see!" she whispered. "Does this have anything to do with your detective work, boys?"

"Sort of," Frank whispered back. "We're trying to prove that Chet Morton didn't wreck the Field Day stuff."

The secretary looked sympathetic. "Chet is a friend of yours, isn't he?" she said quietly. "Ask away."

Joe shot another glance at Adam. He looked suspicious. But Joe was pretty sure he couldn't hear them from where he was.

"It's about Adam," he whispered

to Ms. Chou. "He had detention yesterday, too, right? We need to know if he was here the whole time."

"Yes, he was," Ms. Chou said. "He was right there in my line of sight." She smiled. "Besides, he's been on his best behavior all week—probably trying to change the principal's mind about banning him from Field Day. He's even the one who cracked the case, after all!"

"What?" Frank said.

Before Ms. Chou could respond, her phone rang. "Bayport Elementary, how may I help you?" she answered briskly. She listened for a moment, then put her hand over the mouthpiece. "This will take a while, boys," she whispered. "You'd better run along before you miss the rest of recess."

The Hardys left the office and hurried around the corner. "Did you hear that?" Joe exclaimed. "It sounds like Adam's the one who blamed Chet!"

Frank bit his lip. "I guess you were right about him overhearing us."

"Yeah. Do you think he really believed we suspected Chet?"

"Who knows," Frank said. "But you heard what Ms. Chou said just now. There's still no way Adam could have wrecked that shed."

"Or his loser friends, either." Joe sighed. "So now what? We *still* don't have any suspects!"

"Maybe, maybe not," Frank said. "Adam's alibi checked out. But what about the others?"

"What others?" Joe frowned. "You mean Chet? Come on, you know he'd never do something so rotten!"

"No, not Chet," Frank said. "I was thinking about those two kids I just talked to. One missed lunch, and one was late. We should check out their stories about why."

"Okay," Joe said. "But let's hurry. I don't want to miss all of recess."

It only took a few minutes to confirm the allergy alibi with the school nurse. "Ms. Chou's still on the phone," Frank said, noticing as they walked back toward the office. "Who else can we ask about the doctor's appointment?"

"How about me?" Joe smiled sheepishly. "I just realized you must be talking about that girl Kerri from my class. She got excused a few minutes before lunch yesterday. I saw her get in her mom's car from the classroom window."

"Okay, that only leaves one more alibi to check," Frank said.

"Another one?" Joe glanced toward the doors. He really wanted to get outside before recess was over. "Who?"

"Timmy," Frank said. "He was late to lunch, remember?"

"Only because he was listening to Ms. Walsh blab about fractions," Joe said.

"We'd better double-check that he was really talking to her," Frank said.

Joe sighed. If they even mentioned fractions to Ms. Walsh, she'd probably talk about them for the rest of recess.

But Frank was already heading down the hall. Sometimes it wasn't easy to have a brother who was Mr. Thorough.

"Fine," Joe said. "But don't mention fractions, okay?"

They found Ms. Walsh in her classroom grading papers. When she heard why they were there, she looked surprised.

"Timmy, the new boy?" she said. "No, he didn't stay after class yesterday. Why do you ask?"

"Um, never mind," Frank said. "I mean, we're just playing a game with him."

The teacher looked confused. Before she could ask more questions, the brothers rushed out into the hallway. It was deserted since everyone was still outside at recess.

"Timmy was lying!" Joe said, stunned. "He doesn't have an alibi after all!"

"Hold on," Frank said, stopping in the hall near the office. "There could be a good explanation—like with Chet. We should talk to Timmy."

But Joe hardly heard him. "It all makes sense!" he exclaimed. "Timmy missed the first half of lunch yesterday—right when the crime happened. Then we caught him by Chet's locker. Plus he's new in school; he got here right before the trouble happened."

"Okay," Frank said. "But why would he do it? What's his motive?"

Just then Joe heard footsteps in the quiet hallway. He glanced over his shoulder and gasped.

"Timmy!" he exclaimed.

Timmy walked right up to them, his face serious. "You guys are right," he said. "It was me. I sabotaged the Field Day equipment."

10

Secret File #8:
Case Closed

Y ou did it?" Frank asked. "But why?"

Timmy opened his mouth to answer.

But just then Ms. Walsh stuck her head out into the hallway.

"I thought you boys were outside," she said. "Now scoot!"

Nobody disobeyed Ms. Walsh when she used that tone. "Yes, ma'am," Frank said. Then he looked at Joe and Timmy. "Come on," he added. "We can talk about this outside."

Soon they were out on the playground. Chet, Iola, Callie, and Phil were having a sword fight with pool noodles when they got there. But they dropped the noodles and rushed over right away.

"We noticed you guys disappeared after lunch," Chet said. "Did you solve the mystery?"

"Maybe." Frank glanced at Timmy.

"I'm the one who messed up the shed," Timmy spoke up. "But I only did it because Adam Ackerman forced me to."

Iola gasped. "What?!" she exclaimed.

Timmy nodded. "Adam has it out for me," he explained. "On my very first day, I saw him sneaking off school grounds during recess."

"Really? We're not allowed to do that!" Callie said.

"I know that now," Timmy said. "But I didn't know it then. So I asked the playground monitor if we needed a pass to leave. She figured out what was going on, and Adam got busted."

"So *that's* why he's got a whole week of detention!" Phil said.

"Yeah. And that means he can't do Field Day. He says it's all my fault." Timmy sighed. "He's really mad, especially since he thought he was going to win the big grand prize and everything."

Frank was nodding as he figured out the rest. "So he decided to make you wreck the equipment," he said. "That way he could make sure that nobody else got to have fun at Field Day since he couldn't."

Iola rolled her eyes. "That sounds like Adam."

"He said he'd beat me up if I didn't do everything he ordered." Timmy shot a guilty look toward Chet. "Including sticking those balloons in your locker, Chet. I'm really sorry about that."

"Is that what you were doing when we caught you before?" Joe asked. "Planting more evidence to frame Chet?"

"No," Timmy said. "That time I wanted to put an apology note in there." He stared at his feet. "I really like all you guys. That's why I was inside just now—I was trying to work up the guts to confess everything to Principal Butler."

"That sounds like a good idea," Frank said. "There's just one problem. How can you prove it?"

"Good point," Joe agreed. "It'll be your word against Adam's."

"And Adam's a really good liar," Iola added.

Timmy looked worried. "I hadn't thought of that."

Frank noticed that Chet was grinning. "What are you looking so happy about?" he asked.

"Because I know what we can do." Chet looked smug. "A superspy *always* comes up with the perfect plan, you know."

"I hope this works," Timmy said, sounding nervous.

It was almost an hour after the final bell. Frank, Joe, Chet, and Timmy were waiting in the hallway near the school office.

"I hope so too," Frank said. "Principal Butler agreed to wait to call Chet's parents until after we talk to her. But if Chet's plan doesn't help us prove Timmy's story, I'm not sure what will happen."

"It'll work." Chet checked the watch he'd

borrowed from Phil. "As long as Principal Butler remembers to meet us out here in time, that is. It's only a couple of minutes before detention is over."

The office door swung open. The kids all ran around the corner. But when they saw that it was Principal Butler, they stepped out.

"All right, kids," the principal said. "What's all this about?"

"We know who wrecked the equipment shed," Joe said. "And it wasn't Chet!"

The principal sighed. "Boys . . . ," she began.

"We can prove it," Chet spoke up. "But you have to trust us!"

Frank glanced at him. He really did sound kind of a like a superspy.

Principal Butler still didn't look convinced. "All right, you have my attention," she said.

"Come with us, please," Frank said. "We'll show you what we mean, but first we have to hide."

"Hide?" The principal looked annoyed. But she followed as they led her around the corner.

Then Frank looked at Timmy. "Ready?" he asked.

Timmy took a deep breath. "I think so," he said.

"What's going on here, kids?" Principal Butler demanded as Timmy hurried off.

"Shh!" Frank hissed as he heard the office door open again. Normally he wouldn't dare shush the principal. But this was a special occasion.

He peeked around the corner. Adam had just stepped out of the office. Now he was talking to Timmy in the hallway. A second later the two of them disappeared into the empty classroom across the way, and the door slammed shut behind them.

"Come on," Chet said. "Hurry!"

Frank, Joe, and a very confused-looking Principal Butler followed him to the classroom door. Everyone could hear the sound of voices inside.

But they were too muffled to understand. Chet pulled a water glass he'd borrowed from the cafeteria out of his jacket pocket.

"What's that for?" the principal asked.

Chet pressed the rim of the glass against the door. "It's an old spy trick," he whispered. "If you put your ear to the bottom of the glass, you'll be able to hear everything they're saying inside."

"Look, this is getting ridiculous," the principal complained. "I don't have time to—"

"Please," Frank interrupted, feeling desperate. This could be their last chance to clear Chet's name! "If you just listen for a second, you'll understand everything."

Principal Butler sighed. "Fine," she muttered. Taking the glass from Chet, she put her ear to it and listened.

After a few seconds her eyes widened. Frank and the others couldn't hear what she was hearing. But they could guess.

Joe leaned closer. "I think we just solved another case!" he whispered in Frank's ear.

"Timmy did a great job getting Adam to talk enough so Principal Butler knew he was the *real* guilty one," Joe said.

Frank nodded. He and Joe were in their secret tree house. It was in the woods behind their house, and it was their favorite spot—and where they liked to discuss their cases.

"Yeah," Frank said. "That was smart of Timmy to pretend he was worried about us figuring out the truth. That just made Adam brag about overhearing us talking and getting the brilliant idea to frame Chet."

Joe grinned. "And when Timmy said he was thinking about confessing, Adam threatened to make him do something even *worse* than messing up the shed. That's all Principal Butler needed to hear!"

Even though they'd solved the case yesterday, this was the first chance the brothers had had to write it up on the whiteboard, where they always took notes on their cases. Yesterday afternoon they'd been too busy practicing for Field Day.

"I still can't believe our classes tied for first

place," Frank said as he picked up the pen. "Mr. Jenkins said it's the first time that has ever happened."

Joe grinned. "Don't worry, my class will beat yours next year."

"Don't count on it! It's lucky for you third graders that Principal Butler let Timmy be in Field Day, even though he has to serve two days of detention for what he did," Frank teased. "Otherwise we would've creamed you!"

He was just joking around. Everyone was glad that the principal was taking it easy on Timmy— especially since he'd turned out to be a whiz at the beanbag toss. And Adam got to be a part of Field Day too, but he had to serve one extra day of detention.

"Can you believe Chet won the grand prize?" Joe said. "He's so excited that now he wants to study the whole history of sports and the original old-time Olympics and stuff."

"Yeah. I think that means he has a new hobby."

Joe laughed. "Too bad, since his last hobby actually came in handy for once."

Frank nodded, then quickly wrote a few words on the whiteboard:

SECRET FILES CASE #8: SOLVED!

IT'S FINALLY FIELD DAY! FRANK AND JOE ARE HAVING FUN.

Yeaaargh!

Great job, bro!

Whew! Winning the sack race is thirsty work!

A FEW MINUTES LATER . . .

Ugh! Frank just talked me into doing the fifty-yard dash.

Hey, hands off! That's my drink!

Better mark my drink so everyone can see that it's mine. I know—the secret tree house!

Hey, Joe—it's time for the beanbag toss!

Coming!

AFTER THE BEANBAG TOSS . . .

Hey! Where's my drink?

Is that it over there?

This IS mine! But somebody's been drinking out of it!

Play the Story!

NANCY DREW
MOBILE MYSTERIES

Bring the Nancy Drew experience to life in this story-based gamebook series for your mobile device! As you navigate the mysterious events at Shadow Ranch, you'll soon find yourself in a world of long-lost treasure, phantom horses, rough-and-tumble cowboys, and fearsome creatures of the wild desert. It's up to you to piece together the mysterious events before its owners are forced to ride off into the sunset. Play the Story!

SHADOW RANCH

This Game Book Belongs To:
TOUCH HERE

Available on the App Store

Find out more at www.nancydrewmobilemysteries.com

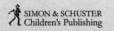

Nancy Drew and the Clue Crew

Test your detective skills with more Clue Crew cases!

FROM ALADDIN • PUBLISHED BY SIMON & SCHUSTER